THE DAWN OF OCANA

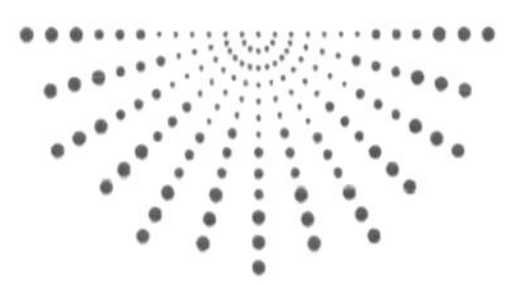

JESSICA KEMERY

Hot Mess
Express Publishing

CONTENTS

1

DARK AND DEEP

Edmond Rizza grunted as the pick ax came down on the stone wall. He felt the vibrations through his arms as the soft coal fell to his feet.

He was a Prince of Vale, a prince of coal and dust, sweat and tears. For generations, his family had wrestled coal and flonium out of the mountain, building their wealth and reaching far beyond these deep caves.

And the Rizzas weren't above the people they ruled. They labored beside them, broke their own bones, and breathed the same dust. One day, he would lead them like his father, but for now, it was his job to learn everything he could. It was his sole purpose in life.

His father, hale and strong, walked through the workers, eyeing their technique and examining a fine line of coal that may lead to a rich vein of flonium, the rare mineral that was necessary to manufacture the fuel cells. With the glowing rock, anything could be powered, from lights to steamships. King Rizza shouted, "Day's done, boys!" His voice echoed through the caves, and the sound of steel on rock stopped.

His father appeared from around the corner, a tall man; he had to stoop to walk through this section. King Rizza's brown eyes, hard and tough, looked over the half-full mining cart nearby and the coal at his feet.

"That's it?" his father said gruffly, his voice hard. "You're slacking?"

"No, Father. I filled a cart right before lunchtime," Edmond said softly.

"Hmmm. Well, you must have been slacking this afternoon, then. Your cart should be full. Why isn't this shoveled in?"

"Sorry, Father. I'll do it before I come up top today," Edmond said, picking up the shovel stuck in the coal pile. So intent had he been on meeting the quota that he had forgotten to fill the dang car. He began working quickly, filling the cart as fast as possible. But it was a big pile. Soon, sweat was pouring off him, and he was panting from exertion.

The men who had been working farther down passed them on their way out, teasing him good-naturedly. "Edmond, still at work? Pick up the pace, boy!" Without a word, his father turned and walked out with the group, leaving his only son and heir working in the gloom.

Soon, it was only the sound of his shovel in the coal, and the tiny light of his headlamp, lighting up the darkness.

Feeling resentful, he gripped his shovel until his knuckles were white, and worked faster as he mumbled to himself. "Always pushing me. Any other man would have left with the others. I should have told him I would finish this tomorrow."

Rarely was a man in the mines alone. He knew the foreman would be at the top, waiting for him, so he hurried to finish. It was spooky down here, and when he stopped shoveling, he could hear little noises in the dark. The drip of water, a cascade of stones, and were those footsteps?

He froze, with his last shovelful of coal heavy in his hands. His eyes strained in the darkness. "Who's there?" he asked, wondering if someone else was finishing up their daily tasks.

To his utter surprise, a young woman appeared out of the darkness. She was tall, with pale skin, long black hair, and eyes the color of emeralds. She was wearing a white dress, and somehow, in all the dirt and coal dust, it was shining brightly. Her hand was raised, and instead of a candle or lamp, a bright shining light illuminated the passageway.

"Who are you? What are you doing down here?" he asked in amazement.

She didn't speak and cocked her head. Edmond was filled with fear. He felt like he was in danger, although he could see she had no weapon. She considered him quietly.

He threw the last shovelful of coal into the cart and dropped the shovel, holding his hands up to show he meant her no harm.

Finally, she spoke. "I know who you are. You are King Rizza's son. A prince. Why does your father make you toil in the caves like a commoner?"

He shrugged. It was a question he had asked himself time and again, but he knew the answer. "My father says the only way to learn is by doing. I'll take over these mines one day. The Kingdom of Vale will be mine."

He wasn't trying to brag, just stating the honest fact, but she seemed disturbed by his words.

"How can the mountain be yours? It's been here long before the fog covered the land, and your ancestors retreated to this oasis above the fog. No, the mountain is mine. I am Atena, Deamon of Vale. You can't claim my mountain," she hissed, her green eyes full of anger. She held up her hand, and the light changed to flames, burning deadly bright.

"Whoa! Whoa!" he said, terrified, as she stepped close to him.

He could feel the heat from the flames, and he was afraid she would burn him where he stood. "You're right! I can't own the mountain! I'm only a steward."

"A steward?" she huffed but lowered her hand. "Then why do you delve deep, cut into its body, take out the lifeblood: the rocks, the coal, the flonium? It's my mountain, and you desecrate it."

Edmond was confused. "Why do you care so much? We need the resources desperately. The other kingdoms, Santiago, Buren, and Nurnan, rely on our coal. They need our enriched flonium fuel cells to power the steamships. Without it, the economies will come to a screeching halt."

"What do I care what the world of men does? My mother and sisters have no need for men. We delve into the mountains, content to protect our domains."

"Who are you?" Edmond asked, fear rising again. "You said you were a daemon. Are those legends true?"

She laughed, throwing her head back. "You humans have no idea. I'm Atena. Some call me a daemon, but only because they don't understand. My mother is Goddess Gaia. My father is Fane, the Creator. They have been here since the beginning of this world."

He cocked his head. "Why have you come to me? No one has seen you before here in the mine."

"Oh, I'm here. Hiding in the darkness. To be honest, I was lonely. My mother pays me no attention, my sisters are preoccupied and self-centered. My father has left again to chase dreams across the stars. I wanted to talk to you. You seem different from the others. I've been watching you."

He felt self-conscious. "Watching me? That's a little creepy."

"And I watch the people of Vale. I protect them. Sometimes, I chase away the monsters who wander out of the fog. I noticed that your kind pair up, husband and wife. And I wondered what it would be like to have a companion," she said, moving closer to him. Her green eyes fixed on him like a predator.

He was at a loss for words. "Ummm. Maybe..." He was going to say something about how he couldn't pick his partner. The World's Fair was coming up, and his father had plans for him. plans that did not involve strange daemon girls lurking in dark caverns.

But his words were cut off as she stepped closer to him and put her hand on his arm. "Come," she whispered. "Let me show you my world."

And then she led him deep into the mines, far deeper than he had ever gone before. She slipped through a natural crack in the rock, and he followed, as she led him farther and farther down, in a dreary world of darkness. So deep into abandoned and forgotten parts of the mine he no longer knew where he was or how to get out.

He found himself enchanted. He knew he shouldn't be here, that this might be dangerous, but he couldn't help himself.

He found himself in a vast natural cavern, lit up by her magic light. Quartz specks glinted in the walls. Here, an old mining operation had been abandoned. He saw rusted tools, old mining hats, and oil lamps strewn about. A stone fire ring was in the middle of the cavern, surrounded by benches made of old timbers. She sat and patted the seat next to her.

"Come, sit and tell me about the world above, on top of the mountain. I promise I won't hurt you," she said.

He obediently followed her directions, blinking stupidly. His body didn't feel like his own, and his thoughts felt fuzzy.

She wrapped her arms around him and sighed. "Talk to me. Tell me about your childhood. I want to know about you...humans."

HE WOKE up the next morning, rubbing his rough hand across his stubble. Blurrily, he got up and went to the mirror, splashing cold water on his face.

Had it been a dream? He recalled talking to her long into the night. Something had opened inside him, and he told her his dreams of the future, his nightmares of insecurity that haunted him.

She had listened intently, sharing her own story of a father who was absent, parents who fought, and sisters who vied for scraps of attention.

And then she turned to him, kissing him softly, her eyes pleading with him for love. He had succumbed to her, allowing her to cover him with her kisses.

In fact, evidence of her enthusiastic attention was on his collarbone. He rubbed the small bruise, shaking his head. He hadn't dared touch her, fearful of his father's wrath should he find out.

When she was done with him, she led him back through the darkness until they heard the shouting of the foreman.

She stepped back into the darkness, "Wait, will I see you again?" he asked with a desperate tone.

"Yes. I will come to you when you are alone. No one must see me. No one must know I exist," she said, her voice fading away.

The foreman came around the corner, holding a lantern tight in his hand. "Where have you been, Edmond? We were worried sick. It's half past eleven. Your father sent a search party down to look for you."

He felt the lie come easily to his lips. "I don't know how, but I got lost. I accidentally wandered into a very old part of the cave and got turned around. Honestly, I was afraid I was done for, but I managed to make my way out."

"Hades, Edmond. Your father would have my head had you

been lost. You're his only heir. No more working down here alone after we are done for the day. I don't care what your father says."

And they had made their way back up to the top. Edmond hung his silver tag next to all the others, the last one on the board tonight.

When he had gotten home, a plate had been kept warm for him. He scarfed it down and then fell asleep, dreaming of Atena.

2
STEAM

Edmond was a steam man. Others liked appa bird racing, and he wasn't above enjoying attending a spirited race, but he had never been comfortable in the saddle. The birds could be high-spirited and took a lot to train and subdue to man's will.

His father seemed to share his feelings, and the Kingdom of Vale didn't even keep any birds, much to the consternation of his friend Gerardo, Prince of the Kingdom of Santiago to the south, who had the finest racing birds in all the land. His family had been the first to tame and race birds, and every year they hosted a race at the World's Fair, hoping to entice more people into the sport.

No, birds were not for him. Edmond would even volunteer to drive the coal transports back and forth above the fog just to get time in the sky. He loved to feel the wheel in his hands and to be in command. He was at his best leading; the sailors, waiting for his call to raise or lower the sails to catch the wind.

In a different life, he would have enjoyed being an airship captain, but he would have to settle for being a Prince of Vale instead.

His father had just ordered a brand new airship, and it was grand. One of the finest ever made. It had replaced the small and somewhat unreliable single-masted ship they had been using for some time. The ship was named The Elizabeth Rose after his dear departed mother. It had been delivered by King Celio of Nurnan from their shipyards himself. It was tied down at its brand-new berth, shining in the early morning light.

His father popped up from below deck, a grin on his face. "This is a fine ship! Your mother would have loved it. She did so much love to travel to Santiago."

Edmond took the wheel, a smile on his face. The wind blew through his sandy blond hair as the ship pushed away from the dock. "Let's see how fast she can go."

As she was fast, he felt the engine's hum under his feet, and at the same time, the wind caught the sails. Normally, he would cut the engines to save the fuel cells, but today he didn't care.

As he drew away from the mountain, his father leaned against the rail, looking down at the city of Vale, the farming terraces bright with color and ready to harvest. The ground below was replaced by the fog, and Edmond swooped low, just kissing the top of the fog, leaving a trailing wake behind him in the mist.

With a whoop, he pulled back on the ship's wheel, and the bow raised, climbing into the sky. His father laughed, holding on to the rail. Finally, he leveled out, looking across the vast distance of the world of Ocaña.

It was a clear late summer day, and the twin suns shone brightly on them. To the south, he could see the abandoned city of Penn, its windowless skyscrapers rising out of the mist from the monster-filled ruins below. The tallest skyscraper, the one with the greenhouse on top, was filled with gars.

Gars were green-skinned, yellow-eyed reptilian humanoids. Sometimes dangerous, sometimes not, they lived in the fog, hunting the monsters within.

It was not Penn that they were headed for, though; they were on their way to meet with the self-proclaimed King of the Gars, Nimmon Gaul. He lived on his mountain in the mist, the only gar to do so, and ruled the clans. He called his kingdom Gatar, and although it was on the smallest mountain, and his "castle" was little more than a defensive shack built out of sheets of tin roofing and bits of salvaged wood, he theoretically held more land, if you counted the land in the mist than any of the other kings combined.

In fact, Nimmon took their salvaged goods and sold them to the humans in the cities on the mountains. Things they couldn't get or produce. Things like metal, glass, springs, screws, cogs, and rubber. He was an important partner to Vale, and his father made the trip often.

Edmond captained the ship the entire way there, enjoying a day out of the mines. Recently, his father had been taking him on more and more of these trips across the fog, and he realized he was being prepared to take the throne one day.

He glanced over at his father, a stern man, made even more so after his wife had died. There wasn't a lot of joy and happiness in their house. It was work, and hardship, and a stiff upper lip. There was no complaining in the Rizza house, that was for sure.

Finally, Gatar appeared on the horizon. The low-slung, long house was close to the fog, the docks just steps from the door. A stream, tumbling from the heights of the mountain, and fed by natural springs and snowmelt, tumbled down, rushing by the house and then off into the fog.

Edmond could spy the green-skinned gars wearing fur and leather. As he pulled up to the docks, they grabbed the lines with their sharp hooked claws, and he could see their long snouts, with their fearsome teeth sharpened to points. They wore appa feathers in their hair, which was long and worn loose. They had painted their skin with red paints, decorating their chest scales with geometric designs.

The gars who had helped them dock the ship did not speak to them, or look at them. It was a relationship of economics only. There was no love here.

But they were quickly greeted by Nimmon Gual, who arrived at the docks. Nimmon looked more human than his clansmen, but he still had green skin and hair. His nose was more humanlike, and his face flatter. He didn't really have a snout, although his lower jaw jutted out more. His family had interbred with humans over the generations and had lost much of the features of his kin.

Nimmon held out a green, leathery hand, and his father grasped it. "King Rizza, good to see you today. And you brought Edmond! Wonderful!"

"Yes, he enjoys flying the airship," King Rizza said with a rare smile.

"She is a beauty! I hope to have my own someday," Nimmon said, looking wistfully at the beautiful ship.

"I didn't come to talk about airships. I was hoping we could talk business," King Rizza said.

"Of course! Come, my wife, Narsa, will prepare us refreshments," Nimmon said, smiling.

"Oh, you got married, you old rascal! When was the wedding?" King Rizza said.

Edmond watched Nimmon's grin slip for a moment. "Oh yes. Well, you were invited, if you recall, but the wedding was last month. It was a tremendous event. My wife is from the Eastern Clan, and all the clans came here, for the ceremony. Of course, it was quite expensive, so I can cut you a good deal today!"

"Congratulations, Nimmon," his father said, slapping him on the back. Edmond quickly checked to make sure the lines were tied and hurried to follow them into the low house.

Nimmon's new wife was thoroughly garish. There was no human in her blood. It was obvious. She had long green hair, plaited and pinned up with a white swamp flower tucked behind her ear. She moved gracefully, carrying a tray of gar bread, the flat unleavened bread made with swamp wheat. Serving it with the red kaffa tea, she kept her eyes down and then exited the room.

"She's lovely, Nimmon. For a gar. I'm sure you will be very happy, and soon, you will have little ones scampering about. Edmond's getting married soon. I'm busy arranging a marriage with him and a wealthy merchant's daughter. I hope to make the arrangements final at the World Fair, to be held in Vale this year."

"Is the girl from Santiago?" Nimmon asked, sipping his tea.

"Of course," King Rizza said, smiling happily.

Edmond remained quiet. He had met Maria at the last World's Fair but had not spoken or written to her since. She was certainly beautiful, but his stomach twisted when he thought of marrying her. Secretly, he held out a hope that his father had forgotten this plan. He did not love her, and he wondered how he could marry a complete stranger.

Nimmon looked pensive for a moment and then put his teacup down. "So, you came today to discuss some materials? What were you looking for?"

"I'll need some scrap metal. Twenty tons. We hit a good seam of flonium and are going to up our production. Nurnan's shipbuilding has taken off, and keeping them in fuel cells is a battle, let me tell you. Plus, the elves seem to have an insatiable need to make everything automated with fuel cells. Oh, and I'm going to need some copper. I don't need much, just for windings, but at least one ton."

Nimmon sighed and sat back. "The scrap metal I can do no problem, but I already made a deal with Nurnan for all the copper I had. It's going to take a lot to go out and salvage another ton. We'll have to strip some pipes out of Penn. It's very intensive work."

"I need it, Nimmon. Name your price, and I'll pay," King Rizza said. Edmond held his breath. If they didn't get this copper, their fuel cell production would stop, and that would be disastrous for Vale. They were hosting the World's Fair this year, and the cost of it would bankrupt them if they couldn't get the copper to make fuel cells.

Nimmon smiled, his yellow eyes twinkling. "Oh, I won't upcharge you, Rizza. But I want an invitation to the Fair this year. A pavilion and a seat at the King's Council."

His father drew in a breath, looking offended. "Nimmon! I can't do that! The other kings..."

"Won't accept me? I know that. I've never been invited. That's why I want YOU, the host of this year's fair, to invite me. I deserve a seat at the table, Rizza. You know it, and I know it. Besides, it will make all this negotiation so much easier if I can just get the lot of it done at the fair, don't you think? I tell you what, I'll give you TWO tons of copper just to sweeten the deal."

Edmond thought it was a good deal and had wondered long ago if Nimmon was a king, why wasn't he at the fair? It was just common sense, he thought, although he knew the other kings didn't really like Nimmon, him being a gar and all.

His father thought for a moment, pursed his lips, and then slapped the table. "Fine. You can come. The others will learn to accept it. Although I make no promises for Amon Tesserect, you know how the elves are."

"I will deal with the elves myself. If they want to ignore me and pretend I don't exist, fine. I don't do any business with them, anyway."

"Well, it's a deal then," Rizza said, standing up and offering his hand.

Nimmon shook it heartily and then gave Edmond a wink.

3

IN THE DARK

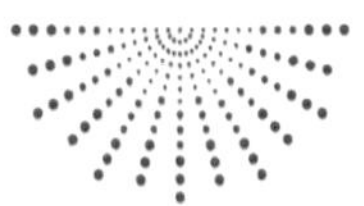

The next few weeks were a blur. As the Crown Prince, Edmond was trapped being his father's errand boy. He ran between the site of the fair, on the gently sloping field between the fog and the keep, helping miners, who had been reassigned to fair duty, set up tents, fences, rides, boardwalks, and the pavilions for each kingdom.

He was in the tent reserved for Vale, helping to get the display ready. Still, two weeks away, he wanted to get this done before the other Kings of Ocaña arrived with their families, and their time would be even more precious.

Their display was simple, really, just a room showing off samples of minerals, a table of mining equipment, and the thing that drew the most visitors, a display of a flonium cell. To end the presentation, they would turn off the lights, and the cell, on a table in the center of the room, would glow with a mysterious green light.

He was setting out the mineral displays when he heard footfalls behind him. He assumed it was his father, come to check up on him or assign him some other task, "One minute, I'm almost done here," he said absently, making sure the placard that identified this rock as pyrite was facing forward.

He was surprised when two hands went over his eyes. "Guess who," the voice whispered in his ear. It was like a song, and he smelled her scent, like earth after a rainstorm and a summer breeze.

"Atena?" he whispered, and he knew he was right when he heard her laughter, silvery like bells. A shiver of excitement ran through him, and he turned to look at her.

She had released him and stood with one hand on her hip. She was wearing a long, bright blue, flowing dress, one shoulder bare. Even though he was no expert on women's current fashions, he knew it was not the current style at all.

"What are you doing with all these rocks from my mountain?" she asked, looking over his display. She ran her fingers over the minerals, and she seemed to stroke them, smiling as she traced a vein of turquoise.

"It's an educational display, really, for the kids. But everyone loves the flonium." He reached under the display table, flipped a switch, and the room went dark. Instantly, the green glow lit up her face, and she took a breath. "Oh, it is beautiful. Raw power from the very earth we tread. But the pursuit of these minerals has torn my beautiful mountain to shreds."

"I am sorry about that," Edmond said, looking guilty.

"Are you sure?" she asked, tilting her head. The green light from the cell made her eyes glow like emeralds.

"I am," he insisted.

"I want to show you something," she said, reaching back down and turning the switch on. The lights, powered by the large steam engine, which had already been erected at the center of the fair, flicked on.

"Okay. I'm about done here, anyway." He shrugged. He had more chores to do, but he supposed they could wait.

"Do you trust me?" she said with a smile, taking her hand in his.

"I don't know. Should I trust you?" he asked, a flirtatious gleam coming to his eyes.

"No, probably not. But I promise I won't hurt you. Or let you be hurt." She moved close to him, and she was intoxicating, like a glass of fine wine with a juicy steak. His mouth was even watering as she looked deep into his eyes.

"Uhhh, okay then," he stammered, a blush rising to his face.

She laughed, enjoying seeing him flustered. Pulling him along, he followed her almost mindlessly until they were just inches from the fog. "Come with me," she sang, her voice carrying on the wind. No one seemed to pay the two any mind, and as the fog closed around him, he had no thoughts of his own safety, only following her.

———

THE FOG CLOSED AROUND HIM, and he felt a moment of panic. It was bright white, but he couldn't see more than a few feet forward. Never had he ventured into the fog before. It was forbidden and dangerous.

In the distance, he heard the cackle of a bau, the monkey-like creatures who lurked in the mist. They were timid creatures if they were alone. It was in packs that they hunted and where they were the most dangerous. But it was a pretty good bet, if you heard one bau, there was a pack lurking, waiting to sink their ferocious teeth into your neck.

"Don't worry. You're so tense, Edmond," she said, laughing. She lifted a hand and made a pushing motion. He watched in disbelief as the fog moved away, revealing a good distance in front of them.

Underneath his feet, a road covered with some kind of black stone ran straight down.

"Where does this road go?" he asked. She pushed again, revealing more roads and a few baus in a skeletal dead tree. The animals looked at them and hissed.

"Go away!" she commanded, lifting her hand again. This time, a ball of flame left her palm, soaring through the air. It hit one of the baus dead center, and the creature erupted into flames.

Howling, the baus scampered out of the tree and disappeared into the fog.

"I hate those things. My sisters, Odessa and Bia, released the monsters when they cracked the earth."

"And why would they do that?" Edmond asked, feeling confused. There were things going on here, magic at a primal level, that he didn't understand. For the first time since meeting Atena, he felt fear.

"They hate the people of this world. Your kind, the ones that tear the earth, deplete the resources, spread their filth. My sisters brought the fog. I didn't agree, but I had no say in the matter. I miss the sun and the green meadows. The city, it used to be filled with life. Now, it's only monsters and hangers-on."

"Where are you taking me?" Edmond asked as they passed a rusting hulk of a vehicle, its hood opened and the guts spilling out onto the roadway.

"I wanted to show you my world when I'm not in the mountain. The mountain gets lonely and dark. Sometimes, I want to see the above," she said, leading him, pushing back the fog. Once, they came upon a startled wild appa, and it hissed at them, but she filled her hand with fire, and it took off, not needing to be reminded of her power.

"This is so strange to think this all exists right below Vale," he said as she led him past a wooden shack. A dirty, rough man, wearing only rags, glared at them from the doorway but made no move toward them. He had an ugly scar down his entire arm, what looked like a healed burn. His eyes settling on Atena and then looking away.

She moved past the stranger with no fear, but Edmond felt his skin crawl.

"It's dangerous here. Never come here without me. That man made the mistake of trying me before," she said, focusing on the fog around them.

"I didn't realize people still lived in the fog," Edmond said. "I was told it was an empty wasteland, filled with monsters that would eat me."

"An exaggeration. It's dangerous yes. But there are people here, Edmond. The ones who escaped the fog were rich and powerful. The ones left behind survive on scraps. Only the strong can make it here."

He pondered that for a moment, thinking, "But Vale was a mining community before the fog."

"That's true, and other places as well, but there is a reason the castles have walls, and it's not to just keep out monsters," she said solemnly.

They were at the foot of the mountain now, and she took a smaller path off the main road, the rocky trail winding around past boulders and scruffy trees. "It's faster to go through the mountain, but you can't come that way." She laughed.

"Where are you taking me?" he asked, avoiding a rut in the road.

Just then, they came around a stone outcropping, and an entrance to a cave revealed itself. It was not that big, and he had to crouch to enter.

Cursing, she lit a lantern, the old-fashioned way, with a match. He was astounded to find a perfectly cozy little home. A bed with a brightly decorated quilt was in the corner, a table with a teapot, and a cast-iron stove, its sides cold, stood near the entrance, its stove pipe curling out the opening.

"How do you keep safe here?" he asked, looking at the open entrance.

"No one bothers me, man or beast. They know better. In the winter, I can seal the entrance with rock to keep the cold out."

"Oh," he said, but that's all he had words for because the next thing he knew, she was leading him to her bed, pushing him down, and undressing him.

His eyes were wide as she pulled her bright blue wrap dress off, revealing her perfect skin, her breasts spilling out into his hands. "Atena..." he whispered, in awe of her beauty.

"Shhhhh, love," she said, pressing against him.

LATER, much later, he lay, caressing her shoulder, her dark hair spilling across his chest. Suddenly, her head snapped up. "They are looking for you."

"How long has it been?" he said in a dreamy voice. He felt like she had cast a spell on him. A spell of sugar, spice, and everything nice. Like a puff of opium, all he wanted was more of her.

She jumped up fast as a cat. She slipped her dress on and then pushed his clothes into his hands. "Dress. Quickly. They are looking for you."

"How do you know?" he said stupidly. He felt slow, like he was mired in the mud.

"I know everything that happens on my mountain," she said, pulling him upright.

He dressed quickly at her urging and let her lead him out of the cave. Indeed, some time had passed, and the fog was dim. She did not bother to push back the fog, instead pulling him along the path.

Once or twice, he heard the chatter of baus. Another time, the snorting of a mega, the enormous horse-like creatures who dwelled in the valley. If encountered, they were likely to stomp you to death.

But they were no concern to her, and soon, he heard calling from the slope above.

"Call to them. If they come into the fog, they could be attacked," she said to him, concern heavy in her voice.

"Oh, so you care about the humans who live above?"

"Of course, I don't want to see anyone get hurt. Even if they do not know it, the people of Vale are under my protection," she said, her voice taking on an urgent tone. "Tell them you got lost in the fog. Do not tell them of me."

"But why—" he started to ask, and she held a finger to his lips. He smiled and asked, "When can I see you again."

"I will come to you. Do not look for me," she insisted.

"Edmond! Edmond, are you there?" he heard a chorus of voices calling for him.

"I'm here. In the fog," he answered, and then he felt her drop his hand and give him a little push.

She was gone, like a shadow in the fog, and he moved toward the voices until he stumbled out into the open air.

His father was there, pacing. When he saw his son emerge from the fog, he let out a huge sob, rushed forward, and embraced him. "My son! I thought you were lost. What were you thinking? Going into the fog?"

Edmond could feel his father shaking through his thick cloak. He felt lightheaded, but the sudden weight of his father's worry hit him. "I'm…I'm sorry," he stuttered. "I don't know what happened. I guess I just accidentally wandered into the fog, and then I got turned around, so I froze."

"It's a wonder the baus didn't get you," his father cried, real tears running down his face. "Come home and rest. You must be exhausted from your ordeal."

And Edmond was exhausted, but not from fear, but the exertion of love. He followed, his head hanging, feeling shame for giving into his desires, while everyone hunted and worried for him.

But before entering the keep, he turned his head to the fog. Was she still there, looking after him? He licked his lips and tasted her.

4

THE FAIR

The airships arrived, their hulks sliding up to Vale's docks. The only ship grander than the Elizabeth Rose was the ship from Nurnan. The Cielos were shipbuilders, and their ship was intended to show off their abilities.

In fact, when Edmond and his father greeted the elves from Buran, their ship was half the size, although perhaps much more opulent. The Elvish King, Amon Tesserect, walked surrounded by his elvish entourage, his serene and cold wife on his arm.

He looked down his nose at Vale. "I'm glad we are staying on our ship. The Keep of Vale is no better than a pigsty," Edmond heard him say to his wife.

But there weren't any rooms to be had in Vale. Every inn was bursting with visitors. Temporary docks had been erected, and for a mile, airships moored onto pilings, sunk just at the edge of the fog.

Edmond was run ragged, making sure last-minute details were complete. An almost catastrophic failure of the goat tents the day before had him rigging up a fix just as the first goats were being led into their pens.

Everyone was talking about the tame appa birds King Zapeda brought from Santiago. The World's Fair appa race was the most anticipated event. The course was small and went over the mountain top and back. It would feature three of Zapeda's golden birds, raced by the king himself, his son Gerardo, and King Cielo. It was being billed as the "battle of the royals."

Even though the crowds were thick, he found himself looking toward the fog, wishing Atena would find him again. His thoughts were filled with her, and every time his father mentioned the closing ball, his heart sank.

"It will be a good match, you and Maria. Her father is a rich trader and a minor lord with a fleet of ships. Plus, she is a beauty that sweetens the pot, doesn't it, my boy?"

"I guess," he mumbled, not meeting his father's eyes.

5

THE PROPOSAL

"Look at this beauty! Such a good bird, I knew she would be the winner," Gerardo said, stroking the golden appa's side. Earlier today, he had ridden the bird to victory in the race over the mountain and back.

Its feathers were the color of honey, and it made a chuffing noise. Edmond and Gerardo were standing in the small appa barn. The three birds the Kingdom of Santiago had brought for their race were in pens lined with hay. After the race, the barn had seen a steady stream of visitors, all wanting to gawk at the birds. Many people wanted to ask Gerardo questions about how he went about taming them, but now the fair was closed, and the barn was silent. The two friends were making sure the birds were bedded down tight for the night. The Kingdom of Santiago even went to the extreme of having the barn guarded twenty-four hours, as they didn't want one of their prized birds stolen by some opportunist.

Edmond stared at the bird warily, holding out a limp carrot. Its yellow eyes stared at him, and its beak was razor sharp. It snatched the carrot out of his hand lightning-fast, and he nearly yelped, pulling back his fingers fearfully.

Appa birds were enormous creatures, larger than a man. They normally lived in the mountain tops, in clean nests lined with spruce branches and feathers. They hunted the slopes, swooping down and snatching up baus and sometimes even humans. "All your birds are golden. I've never seen a golden appa before," Edmond said, keeping his eye on the bird. He was not afraid to admit they intimidated him.

"I know! These are all related to a golden pair we found above Santiago. They were easy to train and gentler than the reds or blacks," Gerardo said happily, scratching his bird under its chin. The bird raised its beak and closed its eyes. It apparently liked that.

"I don't know, my friend. Why would you want to ride one? We have perfectly good airships," Edmond argued, still not sold on the idea.

"Because it's fun! Besides, it's so much easier to get in and out of the goat ranges with a bird, and they help protect the animals from baus and other appas."

"If you say so," Edmond said, unwilling to admit his friend might have a point.

"I've ridden them before. There is nothing else like riding an appa," a quiet voice behind them said.

Both the young men turned, and behind them was Maria Hernandez, daughter of a minor lord of Santiago. She had long black hair piled on her head, sparkling blue eyes, and high fine cheekbones. She wore a silk dress lined in black lace with a matching shawl over her shoulders.

She had come with her family to the fair not only to partake in its delights but to meet the young Prince of Vale, to whom she was to be married.

"Maria, hello," Gerardo said, kissing her hand. She blushed and fluttered her eyelashes.

"Queen Elenor sent me to find you, Gerardo," she said, smiling. "She wants you to know it's almost time for dinner."

"Of course, I'll head back to our airship now," Gerardo said, and then he turned to Edmond, attempting to explain his unexpected familiarly, "Maria is a good friend and frequent guest of the palace. She's been serving as a lady-in-waiting to my mother."

Edmond was struck silent, as he had been this entire fair. He had only spoken a few words to her at the opening dinner. Earlier today, she had sat by him at the race, and he could barely make small talk. Tomorrow was the ball, and she would be on his arm, and it would be announced they would be married in spring. He knew he needed to say something, anything, so he wouldn't appear to be an idiot.

"Hello Maria," he managed to get words to form. "You like to ride appas?"

"Oh yes. It's quite delightful. Gerardo and his father have taken me out for little rides," she said, looking between the two men.

Gerardo looked down, checking the latch on the gate to the stall. The three stood in awkward silence. "She's an excellent rider," he added.

"Would you like to go for a walk? The sunset is beautiful over the mountains of Vale. The moons will be full tonight. Such a lovely mountain, almost dainty compared to the range of Santiago," she said with a smile.

"Of course, m'lady," Edmond said, offering her his arm and nodding goodbye to his friend, who just looked away.

The pair walked arm and arm down the boardwalk. The steam engine in the middle of the fairground powering the carousel chugged loudly over the sounds of the crowd. The twin suns hung in the sky. In about an hour, it would be dark, and the lights would come on, illuminating the games, small rides, and food pavilions.

He cleared his throat, feeling awkward. "Maria, would you like to get a treat?" he asked, gesturing toward a food cart.

"Oh, that would be lovely," she gushed. He walked over to the cart and ordered them two brown sugar toffees on sticks. He pushed a few coins to the vendor. They were quite pricey, as sugar had to be refined from canes found in the lowland swamps, harvested by the gars, and traded to the cities above, but it was worth it. The toffee melted in his mouth.

They walked in silence, and finally he said, "Do you think you'll enjoy living here in Vale?"

She looked up at the keep, at the meadows that surrounded it, now filled with the fair. "It's a wild place on the edge of civilization. It's…quaint," she said, sounding uncertain.

"It just needs a woman's touch," he explained, worried she wouldn't like it. "My mother's been gone a while now, and my father and I don't care much for decoration. But we would have our own little apartment, separate from the keep, and away from my father. We could make it our own. I'll be busy in the mines, of course, but you can run the keep and the household," he went on, thinking about the marriage. He had to admit, in the back of his mind, he felt guilty. He had been imagining Atena in this role. He dreamed of coming home every night, after a hard day in the mines, to her. Or pouring over books and making important decisions like his father with her by his side.

Her smile faltered for a moment, and she looked unsure herself. "That sounds…pleasant," she said. "Maybe I could get an appa bird? So I could fly around Vale? We could get a matched pair, and you could join me?"

"Yes!" If it made her happy, he would agree to anything. "Have you seen our airship?"

"Oh yes. It's beautiful. One of the nicest. I've been on my father's ships, but those are just traders," she gushed.

They walked and chatted a while longer, and then he delivered her to the keep, where she was an honored guest with her family, staying in one of their few guest rooms. "Goodnight, Lady Hernandez. I'll see you at the ball tomorrow, if not before." He bowed low and kissed her hand.

She blushed and hurried off to the keep.

Making his way back to his apartments, he sighed. If he was being honest, he didn't want to marry Maria Hernandez. She was nice and beautiful, but Atena...

"Who was that?" he heard a voice, and he turned and saw the woman he had been thinking of behind him, her dark hair loose and her green eyes sparking with anger.

"Atena..." he said, blinking, "How do you do that? You're always sneaking up on me?"

"Answer my question," she demanded, tossing her hair.

"That is Maria Hernandez of Santiago. We are to be married in the spring," he admitted sheepishly.

"Really? Humm," Atena said, and then she took his hand and pulled him along.

"Where are you taking me?" he protested. She seemed to have a plan in mind. He was led off the main thoroughfare, between two tents, and then away from the keep into the green meadow beyond.

"You seem to like birds. You and your friend spent a long time talking about them. I watched the race today. It was very exciting. It got me thinking about appas and how they live up on the peaks," Atena said. They were moving up now, scrambling up a path covered with loose rocks.

"Atena. The sun is setting," he protested, but for some reason, he kept following her.

"I know. Do you have anywhere to be?" she asked.

"Uh, no. Not tonight. My father will just assume I'm with Maria or Gerardo," he admitted.

"That's what I thought. Why don't we have a little fun, huh?" she said, continuing to lead him up.

"This seems crazy, climbing a mountain in the dark. What if we get attacked by appas? They nest up here," he said.

"I know. That's the point." She laughed. They climbed as the suns set, the sky turning orange, red, and purple in the west. Eventually, they reached a ledge, and with a start, Edmond realized there was an appa nest in front of them.

He saw a white head peek out. It was an appa bird, looking at them with fierce eyes. It let out a screech and raised up, its wings spread.

"Oh, stop," Atena said, holding out her hand. It glowed yellow, and it surrounded the bird. The bird stepped out of its nest, its eyes never leaving her.

"What are you doing?" he asked, his voice low. He was afraid. He had seen men, with their guts spilling out, who had been attacked by appas. They were not to be trifled with.

"I'm using my magic to calm it," she said, reaching the bird. It looked at her, blinked its eyes, and closed its wings.

"Your insane," he said, hanging back.

"No, that's my mother," was all she said. She began to hum, and the bird rocked and sat in front of her, its eyes closed in ecstasy. "Nice bird. Good bird," she cooed, petting its head.

"You made friends with an appa?" he said in disbelief. Not even Gerardo's birds had seemed so calm and docile.

"OH, she's going to let us ride her, aren't you, girl? You're a good girl," Atena cooed, rubbing the bird's head. The bird let out a satisfied little cluck, and Edmond watched in amazement as Atena climbed on its back, smiling at him.

"Don't you need a saddle?" he asked.

"No. Join me. This is a big bird. It should be able to hold both of us for a short flight." She held out her hand.

Feeling incredibly bold, he shrugged. "What the heck. You only live once." But it didn't stop him from feeling like a target. The back of his neck bristled, and he felt shaky as he climbed on the back of the bird, settling behind Atena. His hands automatically went around her waist.

"Up!" she commanded the bird, and it leapt off the ledge, its wings outstretched to catch the wind.

They dropped like a rock, and Edmond thought he was going to be sick as his stomach protested. Straight down, they flew, and for sure, he thought this was the end, closing his eyes.

The bird's wings found the air, swooping hundreds of feet into the air. They circled around the fair. While they had been climbing, the lights had come on below them, and they could just make out the fair guests, riding the Ferris Wheel and carousel.

"Should we fly over the fog?" she asked as her hair flew into his face.

"No. I don't think that's a good idea," he said, "We might be spotted by an airship coming or leaving the fair."

Her lip stuck out in a pout. "Fine, then we will tour my mountain then!" she said, pressing her knees into the bird.

He felt the bird moving under him, and he held tighter to Atena's waist. They turned to the left, and he felt a moment of panic. Surely, he would fall off to his death. They flew over the top of the mountain, and the last rays of the day lit up the top. It was the last days of summer, and the snow had not returned. The bird circled the summit. "I've never been to the summit," he admitted sheepishly.

"It's a good view," she said, and the next thing he knew, they were circling down. The bird landed with a soft thump.

Edmond didn't have to be told twice. He scrambled off the bird, happy to feel the rock under his feet.

Atena joined him, wrapping her arms around him and laying her head on his shoulder. "It's beautiful. This is one of my favorite places."

"It's cold," he admitted, "But lovely. Just like you."

She sighed, looking out at the lights below her. "It's impossible. We can't be together. You are marrying that girl, and I am Atena, youngest daughter of Gaia, goddess of Ocaña."

"I don't know what that means. Who is your father?"

"Fane," she said with a sigh.

"I don't know him." He shrugged. "But he must be important if he married a goddess."

"You don't understand. I have three sisters, Odessa, Bia, and Rhea. My father gave us our powers, and each of us has our own mountains. Odessa has Nurnan, Bia was given Gatar, Rhea roams the hills of Santiago, and I have made Vale my beloved home."

"I don't understand, but I still love you," he admitted. Why must he marry Maria, who he barely knew? If he was being honest, he barely knew Atena, but they shared a passion, and that was enough.

She looked around and spied an appa nest just below the summit. "We have something I have not experienced, a connection. I never thought I would find a friend here," she said sadly.

"I hope we are more than friends," he said. "Maybe after I am married, we can still see each other?"

She looked pensive and then said, "I don't think so." She made her way down the steep slope, and Edmond followed her blindly, not thinking of safety. One wrong step and he would go tumbling down into the valley below.

"Here," she said, climbing into the appas nest. "I'll admit I found this earlier. Appas nests are very clean. I even left a blanket."

"What?" he asked, stupidly, not realizing her intention, until she slipped her dress over her head and put her hand on his belt, giving him a shy smile.

"Come, Edmond. Let me show you the world," she said, leaning back and filing her palms with her power. The spell that intoxicated him so.

Feeling like his body wasn't his own, he moved over her, his eyes locked on to hers. The air between them crackled with power and passion as they came together, desperate for each other's touch.

It was like he couldn't move. When she was done with him, he lay back, feeling the soft feathers that lined the massive nest, cradling his body. The appa bird they had ridden on stayed on the summit, tucked its wings under its body, and waited, seeming to be a sentinel to the lovers below.

The wool blanket was scratchy under him. The two moons shone down on them and made her skin glow like alabaster. She leaned down and pulled another wool blanket over them, covering their bodies against the chill.

He said nothing. There were no words. She was everything to him, but like a ghost, he knew she would disappear for days or weeks until she felt the need for his company again. She was everything he wanted and nothing he could have.

"Marry me," he said, his voice breaking the spell. The full moon lit up her full lips. He rested his hand on the curve of her hip, and she moved closer.

"Marriage is for mortals," she whispered.

"What? Your immortal?" He laughed.

"Well, I guess I could be killed. I am flesh and bone like you, but I don't age. I am far older than you. I have been here on my mountain for generations. I was here before the fog," Atena said, tracing his chin with her finger.

He was flabbergasted; he had no idea. "And I'm your first... friend?" he asked. He had no way to describe what they were to each other.

"Yes, you are my first. Mother doesn't approve of us 'befriending the locals,' as she calls it."

"No, she doesn't. She's not going to like this," an unknown voice, hard and cold, said.

Atena gasped, covering Edmond with the blanket. In the shadows above the nest, he had just a moment to see a dark form.

"Odessa! Why are you here?" Atena cried, pushing Edmond down.

"Oh sister, stop trying to hide your little boy toy. I see him there, naked as the day he was born," the cold voice said.

Atena visibly slumped, and a sigh left her. Emond sat up and looked around for his clothing. It was on the edge of the nest, in danger of being blown off the side of the mountain. He started dressing, staring at the shadowy figure looming above them.

"Please, don't tell Mother. She will be upset," Atena said, and Edmond saw she looked frightened.

"Oh, I'm going to tell her. Little Atena, who can do no wrong, has finally done something naughty. Very naughty." Odessa threw her head back and laughed, and Edmond saw Atena's sister looked a lot like her, but the moonlight on her face highlighted a cruel sneer, not the lovely face he had grown to love.

"Atena, pay her no mind. Come back to Vale with me, be my wife," he pleaded, taking her hands and forcing her to look at him.

She turned away, refusing to look at him. "I can't, Edmond. I'm sorry."

"Take the boy home, Atena," her sister demanded.

Edmond watched in disbelief as the woman sunk into the rock she had been standing on and disappeared. "Where did she go?" he asked, his eyes wide.

"Oh, Edmond. I told you, we are not like you. My sisters and I, we can travel through the rock just as easy as you can air."

They finished dressing in the cold night, Atena folding the two blankets and whistling through her teeth. The white appa bird appeared again, its white head bobbing up from where it was resting.

He climbed aboard, holding her closely. They flew back in silence, neither daring to voice their thoughts on what had just happened.

The bird landed with a soft thump just outside the fair, which was now dark and closed. Not far away, the docks of airships floated, soft lights spilling from their windows as they floated just off the layer of fog.

"Hurry home, Edmond," Atena said softly as he slipped off the bird.

"I'll see you again, won't I?" he asked, hating the desperation in his voice.

She said more with silence than she ever could with words. He watched her fly away, his heart breaking in two.

6
BLOW

The keep was quiet. In the darkness, he could see the torches on the wall, lighting up the guard's faces. Shoulders slumped, he turned toward the main gate.

He made it all the way back to his quarters without being challenged, slipping into his dark bedroom with a sigh of relief. He slipped off his shoes, but then jumped as he heard a match strike.

His father was sitting in his chair by the fire, dressed for bed in his quilted silk robe, his nightcap perched on his head. He leaned over and touched the match to the wick on the oil lamp. The warm glow lit his angry face. "Where have you been?" his father demanded.

"Out," Edmond said cautiously.

"But not with Maria?" his father asked, anger in his voice.

"No," Edmond said, avoiding his father's eyes as he stood near the door.

His father stood and brushed off his legs. "Son. I'm going to ask you, were you with someone else this evening? A girl? There have been whispers amongst the servants and guards."

"And what are they saying?" he asked, fear clutching at his chest, his feet glued to one spot.

"They say that you have been seen with a strange girl. The one that hides in the mist. The villagers call her a daemon woman. They said they saw you in the appa barn and walking together in the fair. What do you say to these accusations?" His father walked closer to him, and Edmond could see the old man was livid. His face was red, and his fist bunched.

"It's true," Edmond whispered, hanging his head. "I love her."

The silence hung thick around them as his father stared daggers at his son. Then, in a blink of an eye, he slapped Edmond so hard across the face that his ears rang.

Edmond clutched his cheek, blinking back tears. When he was young and disobedient, his father would use his belt as a firm reminder he was not to be crossed. But Edmond was too old to be placed across his father's knee.

"After all I have done for you. You ungrateful, unworthy, entitled boy," his father spat, grabbing Edmond's shirt collar and shaking him until his teeth rattled in his head.

"Father. I'm sorry, but I can't marry Maria Hernandez. We don't love each other. Call the betrothal off." Edmond was feeling reckless, hopeless, and helpless. A wholly dangerous combination, he realized.

"If you don't marry Maria, this kingdom and everything I have built will fail. You don't realize the thin margins we operate under, boy. She is the only daughter of a rich, elderly trader. When he dies, the fortune will go to her husband." His father shook him again, his hands like iron around Edmond's neck.

"I won't marry her. If you make me, I'll…I'll run away into the fog," he said, sounding desperate and foolish. But he didn't care.

"The threats of a child. You will marry her if I have to drag you to the altar myself. DO YOU UNDERSTAND!" With the last words, he hit Edmond again, this time with his closed fist. His father's hands, hardened by years of working in the mines, were like stone. When it connected, Edmond went stumbling back.

But now, he was angry. He was not some little boy to be punished by his father for daring to love another. He was a man. Clenching his fists, he rose to his full height, no longer cowering. He had a good two inches on his father, and his arms and shoulders were thick with muscles. With rage, he roared, lunged forward, and grabbed his father by his robe.

His father grappled with him but could not break his son's grip. "Listen here, you old man. I am your son and your heir. I have respected you and done everything you have asked. But marrying Maria Hernandez is too much. I will not do it. Do YOU understand?" Edmond said, giving his father a shake of his own.

The old man looked fearful. Edmond felt his rage subside and let go of his father's robe. The man physically seemed to shrink as the son stood over him, his cheek throbbing. Reaching up, he touched it and winced. "I'll have a black eye tomorrow. Send my regrets to Maria and let her know I won't be able to make the ball. I'm sure you can break the betrothal before they leave the next day."

His father was too stunned for words. "You have never dared to raise a hand against me. How could you? I am your king!"

"You are not my king; you are only my father. Now, leave me be. I'm sorry we fought," Edmond said as tears dripped down his face. He went over to his armchair and sat, looking out the window at the two full moons and the stars in the sky.

"You are making a huge mistake," his father said, looking at him coldly. Then, he retied his robe, which had come undone in the struggle, and left the bedroom.

Edmond just stared out the window. It was much later when he started to cry soundlessly, the tears streaming down his bruised face.

7

STORM

Atena flew to her cave, her eyes stinging with tears. She landed in front of the door and then released the white appa bird to freedom.

Once inside, she filled her stove with a few sticks of wood and used her magic to light the fire. She brewed up some tea and sat on her bed cross-legged, thinking.

Her sister, Odessa, was probably halfway to Buren now, the mountain where her mother lived. Her older sister loved to stir the pot, causing drama between the sisters. Odessa had a cruel streak, whether because she was forced to mother her younger sisters or she had just been born that way. She enjoyed bullying them all.

Atena solved this problem by staying away. It wasn't like her mother even noticed she was gone or never visited. Gaia was a self-absorbed woman who spent much of her time talking to the Elves, telling them pieces of the future for coin she could spend on luxuries.

But this problem was too big. If Atena didn't go to her mother first, her mother would come to her and, in her anger, might take it out on Edmond or Vale.

Sighing, she placed her now empty mug on the table and looked toward the opening. Then she sank into the earth. It would be faster to travel this way, through the very ground itself, than by bird or foot.

Gaining speed as she traveled, she avoided the long-forgotten underground tunnels of men, as they were filled with monsters. It slowed her down to travel through the rock and earth with her magic this deeply. She wanted to avoid unnecessary confrontation. Twice, she diverted for underground rivers, not because she couldn't just move through them, but because she didn't want to get wet.

Finally, she reached Buren, and she rose from the ground near the path that led to her mother's home, just outside the city. It had been a long time since she had been home to the mountain of her birth and seen the rich pine forests that lined the slopes.

The city, with its elegant buildings and soaring spires, was like she had never left. She blinked back tears, remembering how she and Rhea used to roam through the city freely, exploring every nook and cranny.

Setting her shoulders, she slipped back into the earth and headed directly to her mother's small house, perched just below the summit, between the two peaks. It mirrored the city's architecture, with graceful lines of timber, elaborate carvings, and lushly furnished. One perk of having the king's trust.

Popping up from the earth just outside the door, she heard Odessa's grating voice. "Atena has gone and done it, Mother. I caught her with a man, the Prince of Vale, no less."

Atena heard her mother speak but couldn't make out the words. Setting her shoulders, she flung open the door. "Spreading gossip again, Odessa? Don't you have something else to do, like bullying our sister Bia to do your dirty work?"

Odessa shot her a dirty look. "I knew you would come. Let's see how to get out of this."

"Odessa. Please leave. I will speak to Atena alone," Gaia said in her low, deep voice.

"Fine. I hope you punish her well and good," Odessa spat and sank to the floor.

Atena took a deep breath to calm her nerves and looked at her mother, sitting in an overstuffed chair in front of the fire with her bare feet propped up on a footrest. An enormously large woman, she wore a turquoise flowing robe. She had a half dozen rings of varying colors on her fingers, which were bigger than sausages. A large gold chain hung with an amber pendant nearly the size of Atena's fist nestled between her breasts. Her white hair was twisted up, held with a silver hair clasp.

"Daughter, is this story true?" Gaia said, her jowls and chins turning into a frown as she set her own green eyes on her daughter.

Atena lifted her chin, refusing to feel remorse. "Yes. It is true."

Her mother shook her head and stared at the fire, unblinking. The silence stretched out. Atena dared not interrupt her because her mother, Goddess of Ocaña, could see glimpses of the future.

Finally, the spell was broken, and Gaia stood with great difficulty, swinging her feet down to plant into the floor. Using the arms of the chair, she hoisted herself upward.

The woman looked smaller than what Atena remembered but no less scary. She knew that her mother's powers were stronger than her own, and she suffered no disobedience from her daughters. "Atena, you have crossed me. I told you girls, when you went out into the world, to stay away from humans, especially the men. They live short lives, and ours are especially long. In a blink of an eye, this boy will be gone, and what will you be left with? Nothing but sad memories. You are a daemon of Ocaña, not a human. Our bloodline runs directly from the Creator, your father Fane, who would be most disappointed in you."

"You were a human once!" Atena said, starting to feel angry.

"I was, but your father chose me. He picked me to be his goddess and bear his children, hoping his heir would be borne. I gave him only daughters, but that is not the point. You have responsibilities to this world. You cannot turn away from them to be a mother to a human child."

"There is no child, Mother," Atena said, her forehead creasing. She hadn't thought about the possibility of children.

"But there will be. I saw it just now in a vision. Get rid of it. There is a tea. Go down to the city, to the healers, and drink it today. Here is the coin." Gaia flipped open a box on a side table filled with gold coins. She took several and passed the box to Atena.

"I will not!" Atena said immediately, her fingers closing around the cold hard coins. "I had not planned on a child, that is true, but I love him, Mother."

"You can't be with him! You are not human! Your child will be a halfling, an abomination! I forbid you from this. If you continue with this foolishness, I myself will descend from the mountain and take care of the problem. Vale has all those mines. It would be a shame if they all collapsed, with lover boy inside."

"You wouldn't!" Atena shouted, feeling her magic at her fingertips.

Gaia noticed and chuckled. "Oh, daughter dear, do not trifle with me. I will punish you so hard you will wish you were never born. I will tear the very roots of your mountain from the ground. There will be nothing, and your magic will be gone. You need your mountain to draw your magic."

Atena blinked back tears. It was true. The mountain of Vale was the source of her power. She drew from its core, and if it was gone, say in a terrible volcanic explosion, she would be reduced to nothing.

"Get rid of the child. Forget about the man. If you continue along this path, you are dead to me."

"Mother, please," Atena pleaded, placing her hand on her stomach.

Gaia took one step toward her, holding out her hand. Atena felt the magic wrap around her, clutching at her, twisting around her body, invading her as it clawed into her. "Should I do it for you now?"

"No!" Atena said. "I will take care of it myself!"

"Then do it. Be done now, and trouble me no more with your squabbles," Gaia said, withdrawing her magic.

Sobbing, Atena turned and ran out the door, running down the path that led to the city, the coins still clutched in her hand. She paused just at the outskirts. She knew the way to the healers. It would be easy for her to get the tea and to do what her mother said. She had always been a good girl, a rule follower. But now, she placed a hand on her stomach, knowing that she had reached the end of her obedience.

She was done living in fear of her mother and her older sisters. She would go and hide in the abandoned city of Penn for a while. She had friends there, humans she could trade with. She could avoid her spying sister and hopefully save Vale from her mother's wrath while she waited for the child to be born.

Her mind made up, she slipped into the ground again and began moving back toward Vale. She would pick up a few things, seal her cave up with rock so that it couldn't be discovered from the outside, and go into hiding.

8

DILEMMA

ine Months Later. Spring.

Alone in the darkness of her cave under Vale, Atena labored. Swearing and cursing with the pain, she did what women had done since the beginning of time. What her mother had done four times. She reached into the root of her mountain, pulling on the bands of power to carry her through the worst of it.

Even a goddess was not immune to the unpleasantness of childbirth. The child arrived just at dawn, slipping out of her body soundlessly but then drawing its first breath and crying with fervor.

Exhausted, Atena lifted the child to her chest, and the baby opened its eyes. Green, just like her own, with fine light brown hair, like him.

She leaned over, picking up the basin of water next to her, which had now gone cold, and cleaned up the child and herself as best she could. Wrapping the child in a warm blanket, she fed her and held her tightly, looking down at her perfect little fingers.

No doubt this child had some magic, but how much was a

mystery. She was the first of the sisters to have a child and who had dared to defy their mother.

She laid the baby in a woven basket, lined with soft blankets, purchased from the humans who lived with the gars in Penn, and then she slept deeply and without waking until the baby cried to be fed again.

WAKING SUDDENLY, feeling something was wrong, she heard a clatter. Sitting up, she saw a bau climbing on her iron stove, looking through her provisions on the shelf above.

Glancing down at her daughter, she saw the baby was safe, still wrapped in the blankets.

The bau noticed she was awake and jumped down, ambling slowly toward her.

"Go away!" she demanded, holding up her hand and filling it with fire.

The bau hesitated, looking toward the child. Atena could see it thinking. It was alone, so she did not fear it, but she feared it would snatch the child and make off with a tasty snack.

She threw a fireball, and it landed just in front of the bau. It scampered back and out of the cave entrance.

The child cried, and she leaned down to pick her up, noticing the blankets were wet and soiled.

Oh, dear, she thought, looking at the blankets. She had a few more in the chest at the foot of her bed, but she realized she hadn't thought of the child making a mess. She had no way to wash besides a stream not far away. And it was cold outside now, a thin layer of snow on the ground.

The child cried, and she started to feed her again, running her hand over her peach fuzz hair.

"You shouldn't grow up here. The fog is no place for a child," she whispered. For the past nine months, she had worried and fretted about how she could care for a baby. She had little money, stealing what she needed from Vale or bartering with trusted humans in the fog with bau meat.

It was dangerous, and she didn't know if she could keep this child safe, just like the bau that had snuck in the morning. That could have ended in disaster.

And she couldn't move through the mountain with this child, at least not until it was older and developed some magic powers. She would be hampered, held back.

A plan had been running through her head all these months. She would leave the child with Edmond. Spying on the people in Vale, she knew he had broken the betrothal with the beautiful woman from Santiago. She suspected it was because of her but had no way of knowing. Well, she was not meant to be a princess stuck in a keep. She wanted to be free and wild and roam the world. She couldn't do that with this…baby.

She had been the youngest of the four daughters of Gaia. Her oldest sister, Odessa, had raised the younger ones. Her mother had been disinterested, at best. Her father, well, he was absent much of the time. Only coming back occasionally.

She wanted this child to have a life she never had. A comfortable life, loved by her father. She knew that if she raised this child, she would stay away from Edmond. She must stay away, or she would be ensnared into a lovely trap of duty.

No, it was for the best. He would have the resources to raise the child and give it what it desperately needed and what she could not provide. He would marry, eventually, and this baby would have a mother who would love her. For who could not love this angelic baby, who was so content?

She stepped outside for a moment; the dew on the grass cold on her toes. Pushing the fog away, she looked to the sky and saw it was a clear, cloudless day. The twin suns shone brightly in the sky.

Above, several wild appas flew, and she frowned. Another thing to worry about. They could snatch a young child up in their talons and be gone.

And then she saw him, the man who lived not far away in the shack. He ambled toward her, holding a knife.

"What do YOU want?" she snarled, holding her hand up. She felt his eyes travel down her body.

"You've had your baby," he said, his voice low and dangerous, standing well back from her. She had run into him before, and only the fact he stayed well away from her kept her from killing him instantly.

She said nothing but filled her hand with fire, ready to set him ablaze if needed.

"I mean you no harm. I know your power, daemon women," he said mockingly. "But what are you going to do with a child? Sell it to me."

Horrified, she looked at him. "Sell my child?"

"Yes. There are men in Penn, who like young ones," he said, licking his lips.

That was enough for her. Her face twisting with anger and rage, she threw fire at him. He jumped back and ran away, dodging her fireballs, before slipping into the fog.

"Horrible," she said, looking after him. Later, she would take care of him for good, something she should have done long ago. But first, she would follow him into Penn and find out where these men were who wanted young children. Then she would burn it down. It brought her joy, being an enforcer. Whenever she found evil, she stamped it out. With a child on her back, she wouldn't be able to do this. She would be weak, a target, just the thing these feral humans in the fog preyed on.

Going back inside, she looked at the child, sleeping. It would kill her to give up her child, but it was for the best. Finding her paper and a pencil, she sat down and began to write, remembering all those years ago when Odessa forced her to form her letters perfectly.

Dear Edmond -

The child is yours, created in our love. Born of my body, I cannot keep her in the fog. It is too dangerous for us both.

Raise her, love her, and be happy. I have named her Bryn.

I must return to my mountain. I will always love her, but she is yours now.

Do not search for me. You will not find me.

Atena

She waited the entire day and into the night, singing, rocking, and feeding the baby she had named Bryn. She looked at her perfect face, so much like HIM it hurt. For the first time, she felt a moment of doubt, but as the day grew longer, the need to return to her mountain became more pressing. She placed her hand on the cold stone and felt its power.

Just before dawn, she warped Bryn in the last clean sheet she had, ensuring she was warm and well-swaddled, before carrying her in the basket up the hill. She walked quietly past the shack where the feral man lived and saw it was dark.

It was hard to trek the path while carrying the heavy basket, and she was worried that her hands were not free. If something jumped out at them, she would be momentarily defenseless. But luckily, nothing was stirring this early in the morning.

Slipping out of the fog near the keep, she walked through the dewy meadow, not feeling the cold. In fact, she was only wearing a simple cotton shift. Although she was flesh and bone, she did not feel cold, heat, or pain.

Well, she did not feel physical pain. Now, her mental pain was rising, and she wasn't sure she could do this.

She neared the gate, and it was locked and barred for the night. The guards were above on the wall, but they did not see her.

Bending down, she placed Bryn in the alcove, where, during

the day, a guard stood. Tucking the blankets tightly around the baby, she slipped the note into the side.

"You are perfect. You are loved. I'm sorry I must leave you," she whispered, kissing Bryn's forehead. The baby opened her eyes. "Now, sleep until morning," she commanded, letting magic flow over the child.

Bryn's eyes became heavy, and she drifted off to sleep.

With a sigh, Atena looked at the stone wall of the keep. She could stay nearby until Bryn was found, to guard her. Slipping into the stone of the wall, she felt the strength of the rocks cradling her like a hug.

She was still watching an hour later as the twin suns rose. A rooster crowed in the distance, and young servant girl awoke in the village, ready to do her chores for the day before hurrying to the kitchen to help her mother with the daily baking.

9

THE FOUNDLING

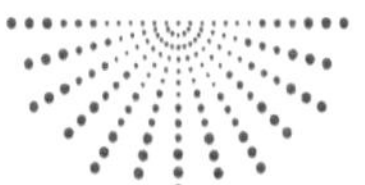

Grabbing her milk pail, the girl named Maura Horn headed down the path that led to the Keep's barn, where the milk cow and the chickens were kept. Her mind wandered when she spied the basket shoved into the alcove near the guard shack. The front gates hadn't even been opened yet, although she saw the guards gathering in the courtyard, getting ready to open the portcullis.

She thought it odd a basket had been left there, and when she heard a little cry, she was even more surprised. Setting down her pail, she hurried over, peering over the edge.

Why it's a little child left at the gates. Who would do such a thing? she wondered. She spied a letter tucked in the side. She opened it and read the message. Her eyes became wide. Prince Edmond was this child's father? Feeling scared she had learned a terrible secret, she quickly tucked the letter where she had found it and looked up when she heard a shout from the courtyard.

"You! Servant girl! What have you found here?" a rough voice said.

"Open the gates. There is a foundling here!" she called back, her

53

voice trembling. The guards scared her. They were so big and carried weapons.

The gate creaked open, and the child cried louder. The guards gathered around, not knowing what to do.

"Don't just stand there!" she demanded, her hand on her hip. Working with her mother in the kitchen, she was used to taking charge. "Someone get Prince Edmond!"

One man moved hesitantly, leaving the baby behind. It was as if all these strong soldiers didn't know what to do with a baby. Sighing, she shook her head and picked up the child. The sheet was wet, and the child was cold. Patting its back like she had seen her mother do with all the other babies, she comforted the infant, and it settled against her warm body.

Finally, Prince Edmond and King Rizza arrived. She handed the baby and the letter to the prince and backed away.

She watched the prince read the letter, his face contorting in pain. The king stood behind him with his arms crossed, an angry look on his face.

After finishing the letter, Edmond looked down at the child and then at his father. "Come, we have much to talk about, Father." He turned to leave, but not before his gaze settled on little Maura Horn.

"Child. You work in the kitchens?" the prince said.

She nodded shyly.

"We will need a wet nurse right away. Ask your mother to send one to me."

"Yes, sir," she said, her voice trembling again. She bent down to pick up her bucket, realizing she still had not done her chores.

"Find someone else to milk the cow. This is more important," Edmond said, and his attention turned back to the baby, who had quieted.

"Edmond! What is the meaning of this?" King Rizza said, his face red.

"Shush, Father. I'll explain in the study. But this is your granddaughter. Her name is Bryn," Edmond said, looking at the face of the child in awe.

HELP other readers find Edmond's and Atena's love story and leave a rating or review!

A LOST PRINCESS seeking to find out the truth. A lonely father trying to save his kingdom from ruin. Can secrets be uncovered before it's too late? Continue the story now:

Her kingdom is in ruin. Her past is a mystery. Will a girl's hunt for the truth end in a desperate fight for her life?

The Suns of Ocaña is the gripping first book in The World of Ocaña fantasy series. If you like complex characters, rich world-building, and dashes of romance, then you'll love Jessica Kemery's newest fantasy tale. Claim your copy here:

ABOUT THE AUTHOR

 Called by some a multi-tasking ninja, Jessica Kemery lives in Crystal Lake, Illinois, where she works a day job so that her dog, Rocky, can live a life of pampered luxury. The Hobbit is the first book she read, and she has been searching for dragons ever since. She has two teenagers who firmly believe their mother is slightly unhinged and roll their eyes every time she starts playing the greatest hits of the '80s. She also has a husband who dreams of becoming her business manager one day when she "makes it big." Powered by caffeine and the bare minimum of sleep on a nightly basis, she thinks the world's greatest invention is meal delivery services.

9 798822 392775